A TINY TREASURE INDEED!

A tiny stuffed pig was hanging on a board next to the register.

It had a squashed round nose and two bright blue eyes. One pointy ear stood straight up. The other ear flopped over.

It was so small! And it looked so soft! Posey longed to touch it.

"Go ahead." The lady behind the counter smiled at her. "Hold up your finger."

Posey held up her index finger. The lady wrapped the pig's legs around it.

Click! Click! The feet snapped together.

The pig held on tight. It felt as if it already loved her.

To Susan Kochan,

with thanks.

—S.G.

To Rebecca Wallstrum,

our own Miss Lee.

I am grateful for

wonderful teachers like you.

—S.R.S.

PRINCESS POSEY

and the

TINY TREASURE

Stephanie Greene

ILLUSTRATED BY

Stephanie Roth Sisson

PUFFIN BOOKS
An Imprint of Penguin Group (USA) Inc.

PUFFIN BOOKS

Published by the Penguin Group

Penguin Young Readers Group, 345 Hudson Street, New York, New York 10014, U.S.A.

Penguin Group (Canada), 90 Eglinton Avenue East, Suite 700, Toronto, Ontario M4P 2Y3, Canada
(a division of Pearson Penguin Canada Inc.)

Penguin Books Ltd, 80 Strand, London WC2R 0RL, England

Penguin Ireland, 25 St Stephen's Green, Dublin 2, Ireland (a division of Penguin Books Ltd)

Penguin Group (Australia), 707 Collins Street, Melbourne, Victoria 3008, Australia
(a division of Pearson Australia Group Pty Ltd)

Penguin Books India Pvt Ltd, 11 Community Centre, Panchsheel Park, New Delhi – 110 017, India

Penguin Group (NZ), 67 Apollo Drive, Rosedale, Auckland 0632, New Zealand
(a division of Pearson New Zealand Ltd.)

Penguin Books, Rosebank Office Park, 181 Jan Smuts Avenue, Parktown North 2193, South Africa

Penguin China, B7 Jiaming Center, 27 East Third Ring Road North,
Chaoyang District, Beijing 100020, China

Penguin Books Ltd, Registered Offices: 80 Strand, London WC2R 0RL, England

Published simultaneously in the United States of America by G. P. Putnam's Sons and Puffin Books,
members of Penguin Young Readers Group, 2013

5 7 9 10 8 6 4

Text copyright © Stephanie Greene, 2013
Illustrations copyright © Stephanie Roth Sisson, 2013
All rights reserved

THE LIBRARY OF CONGRESS HAS CATALOGED THE G. P. PUTNAM'S SONS EDITION AS FOLLOWS:
Greene, Stephanie.
Princess Posey and the tiny treasure / by Stephanie Greene ;
illustrated by Stephanie Roth Sisson. 1st ed.
p. cm.
Summary: Because Posey does not follow the rules when she takes her new toy to school,
Miss Lee locks Poinky in the consequences drawer until Friday.
ISBN: 978-0-399-25711-7 (hardcover)
[1. Behavior—Fiction. 2. Toys—Fiction. 3. Teachers—Fiction. 4. Schools—Fiction.]
I. Sisson, Stephanie Roth, ill. II. Title.
PZ7.G8434 Prt 2012
[E]—dc22
2011006156

Puffin Books 978-0-14-242415-5

Text set in Stempel Garamond
Design by Marikka Tamura

Printed in the United States of America

CONTENTS

THE CONSEQUENCES RULE

"Who knows what this word is?" Miss Lee said. She pointed to the letters A-I-R-P-L-A-N-E on the Word Wall.

"Anyone?" Miss Lee looked around for hands.

Beepbeepbeep!   *Beepbeepbeep!*
Beepbeepbeep!

Someone giggled.

Posey put her hand over her
mouth so she wouldn't giggle, too.

2

They all knew what the sound was.

It was Jacob's new watch. It
had a stretch band and an alarm.
He had been showing it to kids all
week.

"Jacob?" Miss Lee frowned. "Didn't I ask you to leave that at home?"

Posey looked at Jacob. He sat at the table in front of her.

"I forgot to turn it off," he said.

"I know," said Miss Lee. "But I warned you three times. We all remember the consequences rule, don't we?"

She looked around the room.

Posey nodded solemnly. So did the rest of the class.

The consequences rule was serious. Consequences were what

happened when you didn't make a good decision.

Miss Lee held out her hand.

Jacob took off his watch. He gave it to Miss Lee.

"You can take it home at the end of the day," she said. Miss Lee went to her desk and pulled out the bottom right-hand drawer.

Posey's eyes opened wide.

The Consequences Drawer.

That was where Miss Lee put their treasures when they played with them during class.

The rule was that you had to keep them in your backpack. Or you could put them in your cubby.

You could only play with them during recess.

Posey loved to follow rules, but

this one was hard. It was so exciting to share your treasures.

One time, Posey brought her new lip gloss to school. It tasted like real pineapple.

Posey let Nikki and Ava smooth it on their lips. She smoothed it on her lips, too. They licked it until it was gone.

So they needed to put on more.

Miss Lee had to tell Posey to put it away. Two times.

Her lip gloss could have ended up in the Consequences Drawer, too.

Thunk! Miss Lee closed the drawer.

That was the sound of a treasure being locked away.

Posey never, ever wanted one of her treasures to end up in the Consequences Drawer.

DATE DAY

The next day was Saturday. It was Posey's date day with Gramps.

One Saturday a month, they did something special together.

Just the two of them.

"What do you say, toots?" Gramps called from downstairs. "Are you ready?"

"Not yet!" Posey shouted.

She twirled in front of her mirror. Her pink tutu spun out like an umbrella.

She pulled on her T-shirt with the pink mouse. She clipped her kitty clips to her hair.

Princess Posey was ready. She ran

down

the stairs.

"Bye, Mom!" Posey called. "Bye, Danny!"

She and Gramps drove to the hardware store. Gramps needed to buy parts to fix the kitchen sink.

It went *drip, drip, drip* all day long.

Posey loved the hardware store. There were so many things to look at. She and Gramps walked up and down the aisles.

After Gramps found the parts he needed, they went to the paint section.

It was Posey's favorite section.

Hundreds of colors were lined up in rows on little slips of paper. There was every color of the rainbow.

Gramps always let Posey pick five slips. She used them to make art. Today, she picked five shades of pink.

Gramps paid for his parts. Then they went out to the truck.

"What do you say we get a hot-dog and then stop by the toy store on the way home?" Gramps said. "I'll buy a little something for you and Danny."

"Sure!" said Posey.

In the store, Posey saw a small red truck.

"Danny would love this," she said. "He loooves trucks!"

"How about this for you?" said Gramps. "Your mom said you are learning to tell time."

He held up a watch. It had a monkey on the face.

The monkey's arms pointed to the numbers. When the hands moved, the monkey's eyes moved, too.

Posey loved it. It would be so much fun to share. But all she could think of was that terrible *thunk!*

"No," she said. She shook her head fast. "I don't want a watch."

"Okay, don't get excited." Gramps put the watch down. "I'll tell you what. When you're ready for one, you let me know. Deal?"

"Deal."

"Run and put Danny's truck on the counter," Gramps said. "Then go find something for yourself."

Posey went to the counter. That's when she saw the most wonderful thing.

It spoke straight to her heart.

Will you be my friend? it said.

CHAPTER
THREE

POINKY
AND
THE TRUCK

A tiny stuffed pig was hanging on a board next to the register.

It had a squashed round nose and two bright blue eyes. One pointy ear stood straight up. The other ear flopped over.

It was so small!
And it looked so
soft! Posey longed
to touch it.

"Go ahead." The lady behind
the counter smiled at her. "You
can hold it."

Posey tried to pull the pig's squishy body off the board.

It was stuck.

The lady laughed. "It has magnets in its feet," she said. "You have to pull a little harder. Like this."

She pulled the pig off the board.

"Hold up your finger," she said.

Posey held up her index finger. The lady wrapped the pig's legs around it.

Click! Click!
The feet snapped together.

The pig held on tight. It felt as if it already loved her.

And Posey already loved it.

"Looks like you've made a friend," said Gramps.

"Can we buy it?" Posey asked. "Please?"

"I think we're going to have to," Gramps said. "It doesn't look like it's going to let go of you anytime soon."

"Thank you, Gramps."

Posey brushed the pig across her cheek. It was as gentle as a puff of air.

"She's a girl," she said. "Her name is Poinky."

"Poinky, huh?" said Gramps.

"*P* because she's a pig," Posey explained. "Plus *oink*."

"We'll take them both," Gramps told the lady. "Poinky and the truck, please."

WELCOME HOME

Posey held Poinky up to the window on the ride home so she could see.

"This is our street," Posey told her when they turned onto Water Street. "And this is our house."

Gramps pulled into the driveway.

"And those are our swings," Posey said as they got out. "And that's our sandbox. But don't worry." She patted Poinky's head. "I won't let Danny bury you."

Her mom and Danny were in the kitchen. Danny was in his high chair. He was eating pieces of cheese.

"Here, Danny," said Posey. She gave him the truck.

"Tuck! Tuck!" Danny cried. He ran it back and forth over his cheese.

"What a good choice," said her
mom. "What did you get?"

Posey held up her finger.

"Her name is Poinky," she said.
"Danny can't touch her. She's very
delicate."

"Then it will be your job to keep her safe," her mom said. "I hope you thanked Gramps."

"Of course she did," said
Gramps. He put the parts on the
counter. "Now, let me at that noisy
sink," he said.

Posey wanted to show Poinky
her other stuffed animals. They
were lined up on her bed.

"This is Roger the giraffe," Posey said. "And Hoppy the frog. And Brownie the bear. And Kiki the tiger."

There was a doll at the end of the row. It had a soft body and a hard head, but no hair.

"This is Wah," said Posey. "She's a baby, so she cries a lot."

Posey put Poinky next to Roger. One, two, three, four, five, she counted. Poinky made six.

"Who wants a book?" said Posey.

Her animals were so happy! Even Wah smiled.

Posey got a book and sat on her bed. The animals snuggled around her.

Posey knew some of the words. She made the others up.

They all listened carefully until the very end.

NOT YET

Posey told Nikki and Ava about Poinky in school on Monday.

"Bring her tomorrow," Nikki said. "She sounds so cute."

"If you bring Poinky, I'll bring my stuffed kitty," said Ava.

"I'll bring a stuffed animal, too," Nikki said. "We can play a game."

"But what if Miss Lee takes them away?" said Posey.

"We'll only play at recess," Ava promised.

But Posey was worried.

She was still worried the next morning.

Poinky was so small and soft. What if Posey couldn't resist looking at her during class?

She put Poinky back into the bed she had made from a little box. She covered her with the blanket she had made with cotton balls.

"You stay here," Posey said. "I'll
be home after school."

I want to go to school, too, Poinky's face said.

"Not yet," said Posey.

Ava and Nikki each brought in a toy. They played a game during recess.

Posey had to sit and watch. She wished she could play, too.

"Bring Poinky tomorrow," Nikki and Ava begged.

"Maybe," Posey said.

When Posey got home, she and Poinky had a serious talk.

"If I take you to school

tomorrow, you have to hide," Posey said. "You can only come out at recess."

Poinky nodded.

"You have to be very quiet," said Posey. "No peeking or squeaking."

Poinky looked like she understood.

The next morning, Posey let  Poinky ride in the cup holder on the drive to school.

"Are you sure this is a good idea?" her mom said.

"I'll take good care of her," said Posey. "I know the rule."

CHAPTER SIX

A BAD DAY
FOR TREASURES

Before class started, Posey let Ava and Nikki play with Poinky in the reading corner.

First, she clicked Poinky's feet around Nikki's finger.

Then around Ava's.

"Ohhh, she's so sweet," they both said.

Luca wanted to clip Poinky around his finger, too.

"No," Posey told him. "She's too delicate for boys."

"Time to get started, everyone," Miss Lee called. "Maya, put your bracelet in your cubby. I will take it away if I see you playing with it again."

Miss Lee sounded grouchy.

Posey thought it was because of yesterday. Yesterday was a bad day for treasures.

Miss Lee took away Jacob's Matchbox car. And Olivia's paper dolls. And Will's superhero pencil. He kept tapping it on the table.

Posey quickly put Poinky in her backpack so Miss Lee would see she was following the rule.

All morning long, she wondered what Poinky was doing. She worried Poinky didn't have enough air.

She wished Poinky could see

how good Posey was at numbers.

At recess, Posey and Ava and Nikki took their animals outside. They played jungle. It was so much fun.

When they came in, Poinky wanted to see more. Posey showed her the Word Wall.

And the art table.

Poinky loved the crayons. Posey could tell she wanted to draw.

"Ava, thank you for sitting down so quickly," Miss Lee said.

Posey turned around. Everyone was sitting down.

"Posey, put that away," said Miss Lee. "You should have done that when you came in."

Miss Lee was frowning at her.

Posey was so embarrassed.

She couldn't go to her cubby now. Everyone would stare at her.

She stuffed Poinky in her pocket and sat down.

She would be as quiet as a mouse for the rest of the day. She would raise her hand when there was a question.

Miss Lee would thank Posey for being good, too.

THUNK!

Posey worked hard at her writing to make Miss Lee happy. She made her letters very neat.

"Boys and girls," Miss Lee called. "Finish what you are doing. It's time to go to the media center."

Posey loved the media center. When she returned one book, she got to take out another one.

She put down her pencil and jumped up. Poinky fell out of her pocket. She landed on the floor.

Oh, no! Her beautiful pink skin would get dirty.

Posey picked her up.

"Posey!"

Miss Lee's voice was like a sharp stick. Posey put her hand behind her back.

"I thought I told you to put that away," Miss Lee said. "Give it to me. You can have it back on Friday."

Miss Lee held out her hand.

Posey stared at it.

Friday?

But it was an accident. She didn't mean to.

And she only got one warning.

The words tumbled around inside Posey's head. She couldn't say them. She was frozen.

"Ha-ha," Luca whispered.

"You be quiet," said Posey.

"I'm waiting," Miss Lee said. "You're holding up the rest of the class."

Posey made herself put Poinky into Miss Lee's hand. Then she went to the back of the line. Ava and Nikki were looking at her.

Posey didn't look back. She didn't want anyone to see her eyes.

She didn't watch Miss Lee walk to her desk. But she did hear the *thunk!*

Poinky was shut inside the Consequences Drawer.

In the dark.

By herself.

Until Friday.

And it was all Posey's fault.

CHAPTER EIGHT

NO "BUTS"
IN
CONSEQUENCES

Posey didn't want to tell her mom. She would say Posey should have remembered the consequences rule.

Posey had remembered. It was an accident.

"You stay outside with Danny while I get your snacks," her mom said when they got home. "We can have a snack picnic."

Posey sat on the edge of the sandbox. Danny pushed his red truck over the sand.

When he came to Posey's foot, he drove over it.

"No, Danny," she said. "Don't do that."

Danny laughed. He drove the truck over her foot again.

"Stop that!" said Posey.

Danny thought it was a game. It

made Posey mad. She snatched the truck from his hand and stood up.

Danny let out a roar.

"I warned you," said Posey.

Danny grabbed her knees. He tried to pull himself up to get his truck. Posey held it over her head.

"Don't tease him like that," said her mom. She put a tray with snacks on the grass. "Give it back to him."

"He got sand on my shoe," Posey said. "I will give it back on Friday."

"Danny's only a baby," her mom said. "He doesn't understand what Friday is."

"So? Why doesn't he have to learn about consequences, too?"

"Uh-oh." Her mom raised her eyebrows. "What happened?"

The story flooded out.

When Posey was finished, her mom said, "It doesn't do any good to get mad. You didn't follow the rule. That's what consequences are all about."

"But—"

"Sorry. No buts." Her mom sure didn't sound sorry. "Friday will be here before you know it."

Posey went up to her room. She put on her pink tutu and her magic veil to make herself feel better.

Being Princess Posey always made her feel better.

She looked in the mirror.

Princess Posey looked sad.

"It's not fair!" Posey said.
She stomped
her foot.

Princess
Posey still
looked sad.

"Well, it isn't."
Posey's shoulders
slumped.

It was no good.

Poinky was alone in that drawer.
Posey knew she was scared.

It was up to Posey to do something.

CHAPTER
NINE

MAYBE
SHE WON'T BE
SO AFRAID

Posey walked slowly down the blue hall.

What if Miss Lee had on her grouchy face again today? Posey would forget the right words.

She made her stiff legs walk up to the desk.

"Miss Lee?" she said.

"Good morning, Posey." Miss Lee smiled. "You look serious today."

Miss Lee had on her happy face.

"Miss Lee, you put Poinky in the Consequences Drawer," Posey said. "She's afraid of the dark."

"Poinky?" Miss Lee looked puzzled. "Oh. Your little animal."

"She fell out of my pocket," said Posey. "It was an accident."

"It's always an accident," Miss Lee said in her understanding voice.

"But you only gave me one warning," Posey said. "You're supposed to give three."

"That's true," Miss Lee said. "I am."

"You said Poinky has to be there till Friday, but Poinky's only a baby." Posey's mouth got trembly. "She doesn't know what Friday is."

She put the small box on Miss Lee's desk.

"If you put her in here, she might not be so afraid," Posey said.

Miss Lee looked at Poinky's bed. Then back at Posey.

"I guess consequences sometimes hurt other people, don't they?" said Miss Lee.

Posey nodded.

Miss Lee sighed. "Yesterday was a bad day for me," she said.

"Me too," said Posey.

Miss Lee smiled.

"I had a terrible headache all day," she said. "And I was annoyed because so many of you have been playing with your toys."

Posey didn't say anything.

"But that's no excuse." Miss Lee pulled out her bottom right-hand drawer. "I broke my own rule. I should have given you three warnings."

Posey couldn't believe her eyes. Miss Lee took Poinky out of the drawer and put her in the little bed.

Poinky was free!

"Poinky is very lucky to have someone like you," said Miss Lee. She held out the bed. "Put her where she'll be safe until the end of the day."

"Okay. Thank you, Miss Lee," Posey said.

She gripped Poinky and the bed tight in her hand.

She went to her cubby and pushed Poinky to the very far back.

She would never bring her to school again.

She would never, ever, *ever* let another treasure end up in the Consequences Drawer.

CHAPTER TEN

MAYBE SOON

That night, Gramps took Posey and her mom and Danny out for dinner.

Posey had a hamburger and chocolate milk. It felt like a celebration.

There was a clock on the wall.
The long hand pointed straight up.
The short hand pointed straight
down.

Posey stared at it. She tried hard
to remember.

"It's six o'clock," she said.

"That's right!" said her mom. "Good job."

"I'm not so good at the in-between numbers," Posey said.

"Keep practicing. You will learn." Her mom wiped spaghetti sauce off Danny's face.

"I offered to buy her a watch on our last date," Gramps said.

"Do a lot of children in your class have watches?" her mom asked.

"Not too many," Posey said.

"Think you're ready for one yet?" said Gramps.

Posey thought about the wonderful monkey watch.

It would be so much fun to show Nikki and Ava. They would laugh so hard when the monkey's arms and eyes moved.

Everyone else would want to see it, too.

It would be very hard not to play with such an exciting watch in class.

Posey made up her mind. "I think maybe I will be ready when I'm seven," she said.

"You're the boss," said Gramps.
"When you want it, you let me
know. Deal?"

"Deal," said Posey.

✿ ✿ ✿

PSEY'S PAGES

You can make your own Poinky finger puppet!

All you need is: pink construction paper or felt, scissors, glue, markers and crayons, and anything you can think of to decorate her, like googly eyes, pom-poms, yarn, or glitter. Just follow these easy steps:

1. Put a piece of white paper over the Poinky figure below and trace it with a pencil.

2. Cut out the figure carefully. Trace it on the construction paper or felt.

 3. Cut Poinky out.

4. Add any decorations you want. Give her googly eyes or hair or make her sparkle. Don't glue anything on the front of her body because that area will be wrapped around your finger.

5. Put a dab of glue on the inside tips of her feet on one side of her body. (Don't put it on all four of her feet or they will stick to your finger.)

6. Press the feet together and let the glue dry.

7. Slip your finger inside Poinky's feet and there you go—your own finger puppet!

Watch for the next **PRINCESS POSEY** book!

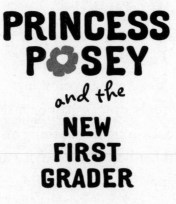

PRINCESS P⬤SEY
and the
NEW
FIRST
GRADER

Posey made up an amazing new game and she can't wait to play it with her best friends, Nikki and Ava. She is going to play the princess and there is a great part for each of them. But when Posey gets to school, Nikki and Ava are playing with a new girl—and the new girl looks just like a fairy-tale princess.